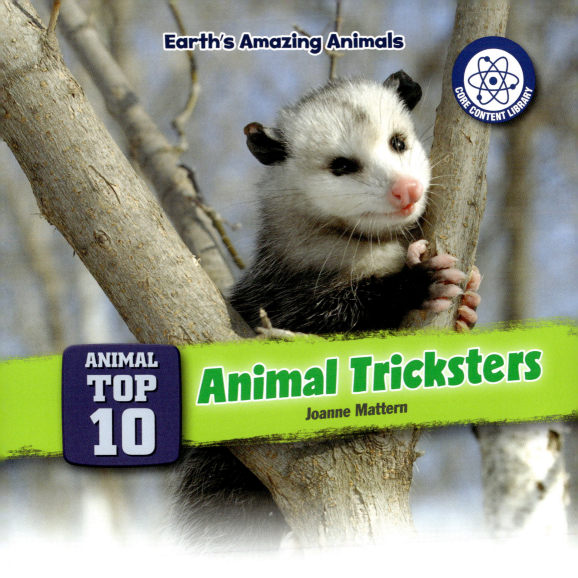

CORE CONTENT LIBRARY

ANIMAL TOP 10

Animal Tricksters

Joanne Mattern

RED CHAIR •PRESS•

Earth's Amazing Animals is produced and published by Red Chair Press:

Red Chair Press LLC   PO Box 333   South Egremont, MA 01258-0333

www.redchairpress.com

Publisher's Cataloging-in-Publication Data
Names: Mattern, Joanne, 1963–
Title: Animal top 10. Animal tricksters / Joanne Mattern.
Other Titles: Animal top ten. Animal tricksters | Animal tricksters | Core
content library.

Description: South Egremont, MA : Red Chair Press, [2019] | Series:
    Earth's amazing animals | Includes glossary, Power Word science term
    etymology, fact and trivia sidebars. | Interest age level: 007-010. |
    Includes bibliographical references and index. | Summary: "You may know
    that some animals play like they're dead to avoid predators. Did you
    know that one animal mimics the sound of the baby of its prey? Some
    animals are really tricky!"--Provided by publisher.

Identifiers: LCCN 2018955619 | ISBN 9781634406956 (library hardcover) |
    ISBN 9781634407915 (paperback) | ISBN 9781634407014 (ebook)

Subjects: LCSH: Animal behavior--Juvenile literature. | Tricksters--
    Juvenile literature. | Animals--Juvenile literature. | CYAC: Animal
    behavior. | Tricksters. | Animals.

Classification: LCC QL751.5 .M385 2019 (print) | LCC QL751.5 (ebook) |
    DDC 591.5/1--dc23

Illustrations by Tim Haggerty.

Map illustration by Joe LeMonnier.

Photo credits: cover (top), 5 (top), 8, 9, 12, 15, 16, 23, 24, 28–31, 35, 36
(top), 37 (bottom), 38 (bottom) Shutterstock; cover (bottom) © Shattil and
Rozinski/Minden Pictures; pp. 1, 3, 5 (middle, bottom), 10, 13–14, 17–18, 22,
25–27, 37 (top), 38 (top), 39 iStock; p. 7 © Fumitoshi Mori/Minden Pictures;
p. 19 © Michele D'Amico supersky77/Getty Images; p. 33 © Emanuele Biggi/
Minden Pictures; p. 34 © imageBROKER/Alamy; p. 36 (bottom) © Doug
Perrine/Alamy.

Printed in United States of America

0519 1P CGF19

Table of Contents

Introduction

Sometimes it's fun to play a trick on someone. People play tricks to be funny. Other times, tricks can be more serious. Think about a spy who wears a **disguise**. Spies have to pretend to be people they aren't. If their disguise doesn't work, they could be arrested or even killed.

Animals play tricks too. But they aren't trying to be funny. Animals play tricks to stay alive. Just like a spy who wears a disguise, some animals know that if they can fool other animals, they can survive another day. Animal tricks can be sneaky and very strange. But they help animals find food or protect them from enemies.

We've put together a list of the Top Ten Animal Tricksters. See why these animals are the sneakiest creatures on Planet Earth!

And the Winners Are...

Here are our choices for the Top 10 Animal Tricksters. Turn the pages to find out more about each of these sneaky creatures.

10. The Leaf Fish

#9

9. The Orchid Mantis

8. The Opossum

7. The Margay

6. The Alcon Blue Butterfly

#6

5. The Cuckoo Finch

4. The Mimic Octopus

3. The Fork-Tailed Drongo

2. The Assassin Bug

1. The Puppeteer Spider

#3

10 The Leaf Fish

What could be more harmless than a leaf? A leaf can't attack anything or eat anything, right? Well, a leaf may be harmless, but the leaf fish definitely is not! This fish disguises itself as a leaf to fool its **prey**.

Leaf fish live in rivers and lakes in South America. Its flat, brown-green body makes it look just like a leaf drifting along underwater. Special fins on the fish's body help it keep its place in the water. Everything looks safe and peaceful—until a shrimp or a small fish swims by. Suddenly the leaf fish's long jaw shoots out and grabs its prey. In seconds, the leaf fish has swallowed the other animal in one big bite.

A leaf fish can eat its own body weight in food every day.

The leaf fish is about three inches (7.6 cm) long.

9 The Orchid Mantis

The orchid's pretty flowers attract bees and other insects. The insects notice the color, but what they are really after is food. Orchids are also full of a sweet liquid called nectar that butterflies and other insects like to eat.

For some insects, flying in for a taste of an orchid will turn out to be their last meal. That's because the orchid mantis is not a flower at all. It is an insect that loves to eat other insects. While most mantises are green or brown, the orchid mantis is white, pink, and purple, just like the flower it is named after. When an insect gets too close, the mantis snaps it up with its long front legs and quickly eats it.

Mantis eating its prey

Orchid mantises live in the rain forest of southeast Asia. There are many brightly colored flowers there, and lots of insects too.

Opossums spend much of their time in trees where it is safe from predators.

8 The Opossum

The opossum might just be the best-known animal trickster. This unusual animal has a simple way to fool a person or animal that comes too close. The opossum plays dead!

Playing dead happens without the opossum even thinking about it. When a coyote, fox, or other **predator** threatens this creature, the opossum goes into shock. It falls over and lies stiffly on the ground. It really looks dead. Usually, the predator loses interest and walks away. In time, the opossum wakes up and goes about its business.

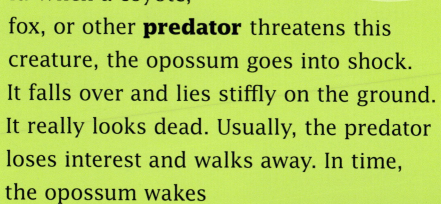

Tricky Fact

Opossums will eat almost anything. They help people by eating ticks and other harmful insects.

Opossums are interesting in other ways. They are the only **marsupial** that lives in North America. An opossum gives birth to up to 14 babies at a time. They are not fully developed and are so small that all 14 could fit in a teaspoon. The babies crawl into a pouch on their mother's stomach. They stay there for about two months until they are big enough to survive outside. After they leave the pouch, the mother opossum often carries her babies on her back.

An opossum's tail is also pretty tricky. It is long, thick, and hairless. The tail is also very strong. An opossum can hang by its tail from a tree branch.

Power Word: *Marsupial* comes from Greek and Latin meaning a pouch or purse. These animals carry their babies in a pouch after birth.

7 The Margay

The margay lives in the rainforests of Central and South America. The small tamarin monkey lives there too. Margays love to eat tamarins, and these small cats have come up with a very tricky way to catch their prey.

The Margay stands about 12 inches (30 cm) tall and weighs 8 to 15 pounds (3.5 to 7 kg).

When it is hungry, a margay will make a noise that sounds just like the cry of a baby tamarin monkey. When the adult tamarins hear this sound, they get upset and rush to see what is wrong with their baby. That's when the margay pounces and catches the tamarin. The cat has tricked its prey into coming right into its deadly jaws.

Margays are great acrobats. These cats live high in the trees. Their back legs are strong and flexible. A margay can hang from a tree by one foot. It can also chase a squirrel down a tree trunk without falling. Its long tail helps it keep its balance.

Margays can run headfirst down trees, like squirrels.

Tricky Fact

A margay's big eyes help it see in the dark.

These cats have beautiful fur, but that has put them in danger. Many margays are killed by people who sell their fur. Margays also do not have a lot of kittens at a time, and they only have kittens every two years. These facts have made the margay an **endangered** species, and even playing tricks may not be able to save it.

6 The Alcon Blue Butterfly

Some animals trick other animals by sight. The alcon blue butterfly uses the senses of smell and hearing to play an amazing trick on other insects.

Like other butterflies, the alcon blue starts life as a caterpillar. That caterpillar looks a lot like the **larva** of an ant. It smells like an ant too. This caterpillar lays on the ground and waits for an ant to come along. Soon, a red ant finds the caterpillar. Since the caterpillar smells just like ant larvae, the ant carries the caterpillar into its nest.

Red ant carries
a caterpillar

Alcon blue butterfly

Alcon blue butterflies live in Europe. The tops of their wings are blue, but the undersides are tan with spots.

Deep in the nest, other workers also fall for the trick. They feed the caterpillar just like they feed their own ant babies. Then the sneaky butterfly plays its second trick. It begins to sing. The song sounds just like one that the queen ant sings. Once again, the other ants are completely fooled. They treat the caterpillar like a queen, bringing it the best food. If there is not enough food, the ants will even feed their own larvae to the caterpillar.

The ants continue to care for the caterpillar even after it develops a hard shell called a pupa and begins to become a butterfly. But when the alcon blue butterfly comes out of its pupa, the game is over. The ants realize that they have been tricked, and they are not happy. It's time for the butterfly to make a speedy exit. The butterfly flies out of the ant nest as fast as it can.

The blue is seen on top of the wing.

5 The Cuckoo Finch

Being a parent is hard work. This is especially true for birds. Bird mothers spend days or weeks sitting on their eggs until they hatch. Then they have to bring food to the baby birds all day long until the chicks are big enough to fly away and take care of themselves.

The Cuckoo Finch lays her eggs in another bird's nest! Sneaky cuckoo.

One bird in Africa has found a way to have lots of chicks without taking care of them. That sneaky mother bird is the cuckoo finch. This bird is so sneaky, it doesn't even have to build its own nest! Instead, the cuckoo finch waits until another bird leaves its nest. Then it lays its eggs in the nest. It can get away with this trick because the cuckoo finch's eggs look just like the eggs of some other birds.

The cuckoo finch lays one or two eggs in a nest. When the mother bird comes back, she can't tell if the eggs are hers or another bird's. The mother bird doesn't want to kill her own chicks by tossing the eggs out of the nest. So she sits on all the eggs and hatches the cuckoo finch's chicks along with her own.

Tricky Fact

Sometimes a cuckoo finch will push the other bird's eggs out of the nest to give her chicks a better chance.

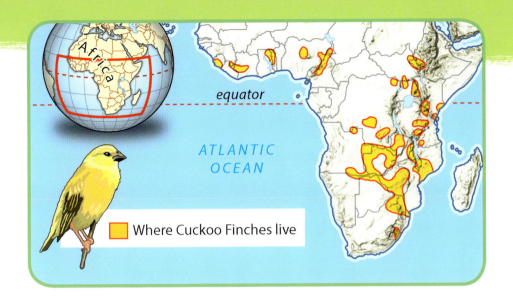

equator

ATLANTIC
OCEAN

Where Cuckoo Finches live

When the cuckoo finches are born, they
continue the trick. Cuckoo finches are usually
bigger than the other birds in the nest. They
demand more food. The mother bird ends up
feeding the cuckoo finches more than her own
chicks.

This trick may seem cruel, and it is certainly
bad news for the other chicks in the nest.
However, laying eggs in other birds' nests is
a smart idea for the cuckoo finch. She is able
to lay many eggs and not have to take care
of them. More eggs means more chicks. And
more chicks increase the chances that the
species will survive.

4 The Mimic Octopus

A mimic is someone who copies someone. It's easy to see how the mimic octopus got its name! This creature loves to copy other animals.

The mimic octopus is brown and white. These creatures also have spots and stripes. These features help them hide on the ocean floor. In addition, like other octopuses, the mimic can change colors to match the world around it. This provides great **camouflage** and helps the octopus blend in.

But the mimic octopus can do a lot more than just change color. It can also copy other animals' shapes and movements.

The Mimic Octopus is small at only 2 feet (just over a half-meter) long.

The mimic octopus can look like an eel or jellyfish.

Why does this octopus copy other animals? Scientists think the mimic octopus is so smart, it can figure out what animals predators don't like to eat. Then it copies those animals so that predators leave the mimic alone as well. This clever trick helps keep the mimic octopus safe.

A mimic might also pretend to be a different animal to trick its prey. For example, if the mimic octopus looks like a crab, other crabs won't be afraid to come near it. But when they do, dinner is served!

Mimic octopuses live in the waters around Southeast Asia. They eat worms, crabs, and small fish. Sometimes they even eat other octopuses.

3 The Fork-Tailed Drongo

Sometimes an animal can seem like it is helping another creature. But the animal isn't trying to be helpful at all. Instead, it is playing a sneaky trick! Pretending to be helpful is exactly how a bird called the fork-tailed drongo steals food from other animals.

Drongos are brave little birds, dive-bombing predators to drive them away.

Fork-tailed drongos live in Africa. They like to hang around meerkat colonies. Meerkats find food by digging up insects and scorpions. Drongos like to eat those things too. But first they need to get rid of the meerkats. To do this, the drongo will make a cry that tells the meerkat danger is near. The meerkat hears the cry and quickly runs for cover. Then the drongo swoops down and steals the meerkat's food.

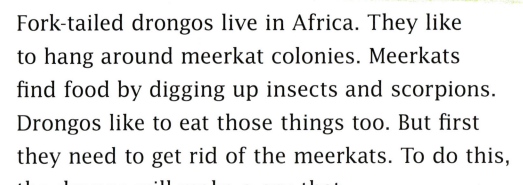

A meerkat catches an insect before a drongo steals it away.

Tricky Fact

Drongos also follow herds of giraffes or rhinos. As these big animals move through the grass, insects fly out of their way. Then the drongo flies down to eat them.

After a while, though, the meerkat stops falling for the drongo's trick. Then the drongo tries a different approach. The bird makes the warning cry of a different animal. Once again, the meerkat is fooled and runs away. And once again, the drongo steals its dinner.

Drongos don't just use their cries to fool meerkats. This clever bird also steals food from other birds and small mammals.

2 The Assassin Bug

An assassin is someone who kills an important person in a surprise attack. An assassin bug also kills by surprise. This bug is one of the greatest tricksters in the insect world.

An assassin bug hunts spiders. Most insects are in big trouble if they are caught in a spider's web. The spider will quickly catch the bug, wrap it in sticky strands of silk, and save it for dinner. But if an assassin bug comes near, things can take an unexpected turn!

Bugs are insects, but not all insects are bugs. A bug has sharp mouthparts. It also has thicker wings than other insects.

Here's how an assassin bug plays its trick. The bug finds a spider web and makes little taps on the strands of the web. The spider thinks a small insect, such as a fly, is caught in its web. The spider crawls out to the edge of the web, ready to grab its prey. Surprise! The insect waiting in the web is not trapped at all. Instead, it grabs the spider and eats it up. The assassin bug has struck again.

Assassin bugs live in Australia. These clever insects have long legs and a thin body. But they also have very sharp mouthparts. An assassin bug kills its prey by jamming its sharp mouthparts into the insect's body and sucking out the prey's insides.

To do this, the bug has to get close to its prey. But getting close to a spider can be very dangerous. That's why this insect has to play a deadly trick.

The assassin bug has figured out how to tap a spider's web in a way that fools the spider. The taps feel just like the struggles of a small insect that is trapped in the web. The spider has no idea that the assassin bug has set a trap of its own—a trap that will end in dinner for the bug, not the spider!

1 The Puppeteer Spider

And now, we present the #1 animal trickster—THE PUPPETEER SPIDER!

One day in 2012, a scientist named Phil Torres was leading a group through a forest in Peru when he saw a funny-looking spider in a web. It wasn't until the scientist got closer that he realized the spider wasn't real at all. Instead, it was a fake. Torres looked closer and saw a smaller spider in the web. The small spider was shaking the web to make the **decoy** move. Torres had never seen anything like it.

Torres told other scientists about what he had seen. Later, he went back to the forest and found more spiders. They were part of a group of spiders called *Cyclosa*.

Cyclosa spiders live in rain forests all over Asia and South America.

Other scientists studied the spiders. They saw that the fake spiders were made of dead insects, pieces of leaves, dried-up frog eggs, and other garbage. The real spider made the fake spider move just like a person moves a puppet.

Why does the spider do this? Scientists think the behavior might scare away predators. For example, the damselfly is a predator that eats small spiders, but stays away from big spiders. Maybe the puppeteer spider makes the big fake spider to keep damselflies away.

Fake spiders are made of dead insects, leaves and pieces of garbage.

Cyclosa spiders weaving an intricate web

Scientists agree that the puppeteer spiders aren't smart enough to figure out that building a decoy spider will trick predators into staying away. They think that the spiders that do this have a better chance of surviving than spiders that do not. That means that spiders with this ability will be the ones that live and reproduce. Sometimes being tricky really does pay off.

Animal Trickster Runners-Up

Here are a few more creatures that didn't quite make the Top 10, but are still pretty sneaky!

Green heron

Anglerfish

Wobbegong

Photuris firefly

What's Your Top 10?

You've seen our list of the
Top 10 Animal Tricksters
and some runners-up as well.
Now it's your turn! Which animals
in this book do YOU think are the sneakiest? Are there
other animals that you think should be on the list? Check
your library or go on the Internet and find photos and
information on all that's tricky in the animal world.
Then make your own Top 10 list!

Glossary

camouflage markings that blend in with the background

decoy a fake object that leads something into a trap

disguise something that hides the identity of a person or animal

endangered in danger of dying out

larvae in insects, the stage between the egg and the pupa

marsupial a mammal whose babies are not completely developed when they are born

predators animals that eat other animals for food

prey animals eaten by other animals for food

Learn More in the Library

Spelman, Lucy. *National Geographic Animal Encyclopedia.* National Geographic Children's Books, 2012.

various. *Bugs (Pocket Genius).* DK Children's Books, 2016.

Index

About the Author

Joanne Mattern is the author of nearly 350 books for children and teens. She began writing when she was a little girl and just never stopped! Joanne loves nonfiction because she enjoys bringing science topics to life and showing young readers that nonfiction is full of compelling stories! Joanne lives in the Hudson Valley of New York State with her husband, four children, and several pets!